AT YOUR AGE, I THOUGHT I ALREADY KNEW EVERYTHING. I PREFERRED HAVING FUN...

BE RIGHT DOWN, INDIANA.

ARF RUF RUF

RUF ARF RUF

THEN ONE DAY, MY DAD WAS INVITED TO A WHOLE LOT OF UNIVERSITIES AROUND THE WORLD...

KRRUNCH

AND WE WERE GOING WITH HIM!

OUR FIRST STOP WAS OXFORD, ENGLAND.

OXFORD. WHERE MY DAD HAD STUDIED. HE SAID HE HAD A SURPRISE FOR ME.

SOME SURPRISE!

MORE LIKE A *SHOCK!*

HUMPH! HIS CLOTHES ARE APPALLING! HIS POSTURE LEAVES MUCH TO BE DESIRED!

MISS *HELEN SEYMOUR!*

HOW OLD ARE YOU, YOUNG MAN?

ARE YOU DEAF?

NINE.

HE MUMBLES.

NINE!!

IMPOSSIBLE! HE'S TOO YOUNG! I AM NOT A GOVERNESS. I AM A *TEACHER!*

YOU'RE THE BEST! HE NEEDS YOU!

OUT OF THE QUESTION.

I *HATE* HER! SHE'S A *WITCH!*

THEN LET *HIM* GO WITH HER!

DARLING, MISS SEYMOUR TUTORED YOUR FATHER! HE THINKS THE WORLD OF HER.

STALEMATE!

BUT, LIKE I SAID, MY FATHER WAS A VERY SMART MAN.

YOU'VE ALWAYS YEARNED FOR A CHANCE TO TRAVEL...

NOT A SINGLE MILE WITH THAT BOY.

THE GREAT WALL OF CHINA, THE GARDENS OF KYOTO. AHH, THE TAJ MAHAL BY MOONLIGHT ...SUNSET OVER THE PYRAMIDS.

MOM AND DAD ENJOYED THE VOYAGE SOUTH.

ME? I MISSED ALL THE FUN.

STILL, I HAD MY MOMENTS... LIKE WHEN THE SEAS GOT ROUGH.

HEAVY WEATHER, CAPTAIN! LUCKILY, WE BRITISH ARE A HARDY LOT, WHAT?

INDEED, BISHOP!

AND YOU, YOUNG FELLOW, WHAT DID YOU LEARN TODAY?

ABOUT MUMMIES, SIR! HOW THE ANCIENT EGYPTIANS TURNED DEAD PEOPLE INTO MUMMIES.

OH...?

YES, SIR. YOU SEE, THEY'D WAIT A FEW DAYS UNTIL THE BODY GOT *SOFT*, THEN THEY'D *SCOOP* OUT THE BRAIN.

FIRST, THEY'D DRILL UP INTO THE NOSE...THEN USE A *HOOK* TO *TEE-EASE* THE BRAIN OUT, *REEEAL* SLOW-LIKE.

'SCUSE ME...

THEN THEY CUT OPEN THE WHOLE LEFT SIDE OF THE CORPSE, REACHED IN AND PULLED OUT ALL THE *LOWER ORGANS*. THEY LEFT THE *KIDNEYS* IN.

NEXT, THEY'D OPEN THE CHEST...HAUL OUT *EVERYTHING* BUT THE HEART. THEY'D WASH ALL THESE, POUR GOO ON THEM, WRAP THEM—

—AND PUT EACH ORGAN IN A SEPARATE JAR. ONE FOR THE *LIVER*, ONE FOR THE *LUNGS*...

AFTER THEY CLEANED OUT THE BODY, DRIED IT AND STUFFED IT, THEY'D TIE ON THE TOENAILS AND FINGERNAILS...

...SO THEY WOULDN'T *FALL OFF*!

THAT WAS THE *FIRST* STAGE...THE *EMBALMING*.

CAIRO 1908

THE GREAT PYRAMID. BUILT MORE THAN FOUR THOUSAND YEARS AGO!

BY KING CHEOPS. FOURTH DYNASTY.

VERY GOOD, HENRY!

IT WAS THE LARGEST STRUCTURE EVER MADE BY MAN, THE FIRST EVER OF STONE, AND ONE OF THE SEVEN WONDERS OF THE WORLD.

VERY GOOD.

·ωὂω· @*!!

MISS SEYMOUR, WHY DID YOU GIVE HIM ONLY TEN PIASTRES? HE ASKED FOR THIRTY.

IT'S QUITE ALL RIGHT! THESE PEOPLE EXPECT TO BARTER.

LET US GET ON. WE WERE SPEAKING OF THE PYRAMID.

KING CHEOPS MUST HAVE BEEN PRETTY OLD BY THE TIME THEY FINISHED IT!

SOME PHARAOHS LIVED TO A GREAT AGE. RAMESES THE SECOND WAS OVER NINETY—

OVER NINETY! GOLLY-GOSH! HOW CAN A PERSON LIVE THAT LONG?

HEY... YOU OKAY, MISTER?

EH? UHN, OF COURSE. WHERE WAS I? OH. YES...

—WHILE OTHER PHARAOHS WERE MERE BOYS, NOT MUCH OLDER THAN YOU, HENRY.

GEE-EE...

MISS SEYMOUR —*LOOK!!*

OH, MY GOODNESS!

HE'S TAKING OUR CAMELS!

HEY, MISTER— *WAIT!*

WAIT— WAIT! COME BACK! OH, DEAR. WHAT ON EARTH SHALL WE DO?

WALK?

IT'S MUCH TOO FAR. AND IT WILL SOON BE DARK.

G- GOLLY, MISS SEYMOUR. WHAT IF WE'RE ATTACKED —BY *BANDITS?*

OR— OR *TOMB ROBBERS?* THEY'RE SUPPOSED TO BE REAL *SCARY!*

HENRY, LISTEN TO ME! THERE IS NOTHING TO BE AFRAID OF!

HOW ARE WE GOING TO GET BACK?

BE QUIET FOR A MOMENT. LET ME THINK.

SOMEONE'S COMING. WE'RE SAVED!

WHAT IF IT'S...A TOMB ROBBER...COMING TO *MURDER* US?

HAVING A SPOT OF TROUBLE?

MR. LAWRENCE! WHAT ARE *YOU* DOING HERE?

IT WAS MR. T.E. LAWRENCE. *THE* LAWRENCE OF ARABIA, AS HE WOULD COME TO BE KNOWN. A HERO. A LEGEND.

YEAH, MY OLD MAN SAW THE MOVIE, I THINK. SO...?

HE'D STUDIED WITH MISS SEYMOUR AT OXFORD. HE KNEW MY DAD'S BOOKS. WE BECAME PALS. AND HE MADE US FEEL SAFE.

NOT TO WORRY. THERE WILL BE PLENTY OF CAMELS ALONG IN THE MORNING.

AND HOW HE COULD TALK— A SPELLBINDER. SEEMS HE KNEW JUST ABOUT *EVERY*THING...

WHAT IT MUST BE LIKE TO OPEN A MUMMY'S TOMB.

YOUR FEET ARE THE FIRST TO TREAD THAT FLOOR IN *FOUR THOUSAND YEARS.*

YOU ARE BREATHING THE SAME AIR AS THE MEN WHO LAID THE MUMMY TO REST!

GOLL-EEE-EE!

I'D SURE LIKE TO BE AN ARCHAEOLOGIST!

PERHAPS YOU'LL DISCOVER A TREASURE BEYOND PRICE!

AND GET RICH?

NO, HENRY! ARCHAEOLOGISTS DON'T *STEAL* FROM THE PAST! THEY *OPEN* IT UP TO EVERYONE—AND MAKE THE WHOLE WORLD RICHER!

WE WENT ON AND ON. I WONDERED WHY MUMMIES NEEDED THEIR THINGS IN THE TOMB WITH THEM.

THEY BELIEVED THE SPIRIT WOULD REMAIN *ALIVE* AND NEED FOOD AND SHELTER JUST LIKE US!

WOW! IS IT *TRUE*?

NO, HENRY! IT IS WHAT SOME EGYPTIANS BELIEVED.

WHAT *DOES* HAPPEN WHEN YOU DIE?

THE *BOMBSHELL!*

FOR MISS SEYMOUR—A MINISTER'S DAUGHTER—THERE WAS ONLY *ONE* "PROPER" ANSWER!

BUT NED (MR. LAWRENCE) OPENED UP A WIDE WORLD OF DIFFERENT BELIEFS...

...FROM THE MOSLEMS' PARADISE...

...TO THE HINDUS' REINCARNATION.

WELL, WHICH ONE IS *TRUE*?!

NED WAS HEADING UP-RIVER TO THE VALLEY OF THE KINGS, THE SITE OF HOWARD CARTER'S BIG DIG.

AND DAD LET US GO *WITH* HIM!

I GOT MY FIRST LESSON IN READING HIEROGLYPHS, THE PICTURE-LANGUAGE OF ANCIENT EGYPT.

The Valley of the Kings

AND THEN, MY FIRST SIGHT OF AN ARCHAEOLOGICAL DIG. IT WAS SOMETHING TO SEE.

NED'S FRIEND, RASHID SALLAM, WAS THERE TO GREET US.

NED, YOU'RE IN LUCK! WE'VE DISCOVERED A NEW TOMB.

OH, SMASHING!

NOT A PHARAOH, MIND YOU. BUT STILL IMPORTANT.

WILL WE GET TO SEE INSIDE IT?

I DO HOPE SO, MR. JONES!

OH, WOW! THAT WOULD BE *GREAT!*

MISTER GHALY—

—WHY ARE THOSE MEN SITTING IDLE?

THEY SAY THERE IS A *CURSE* ON THE TOMB. THEY ARE AFRAID.

NONSENSE! YOU KNOW THERE IS NO SUCH THING. PUT THEM BACK TO WORK —AT *ONCE*, MR. GHALY!

OUR OVERSEER! I THINK HE *FEEDS* THEIR SUPERSTITIONS!

B-BUT THERE *COULD* BE A CURSE, COULDN'T THERE?

OF COURSE NOT, YOUNG MAN.

TWEE-EEEE

STEADY ON. DEMETRIOS IS GOING TO BLOW UP A ROCK!

ALL CLEAR DOWN HERE, DEMETRIOS!

YOU MAY COVER YOUR EARS, MISS SEYMOUR.

P-WHOOM

IMSHI! *IMSHI!*

WHOOSH

ALL SAFE NOW.

POO·OOF

HE'S RECORDING OUR RECENT FINDS. POTTERY, LINEN, CLAY SEALS.

THIS ONE BEARS THE NAME: TUT-ANKH-AMEN.

THE BOY-PHARAOH, MR. CARTER?

BOY-PHARAOH?

THE TOMB WE FOUND YESTERDAY— THE CHAP'S NAME WAS *KHA*— WE'RE ABOUT TO OPEN IT. CARE TO COME ALONG?

JEEPERS, MISTER CARTER. *WOULD I!!*

YES, MR. JONES— ABOUT EIGHTEEN WHEN HE DIED. ABOUT *YOUR* AGE WHEN HE BECAME KING. ONE DAY, YOUNG MAN, I HOPE TO UNCOVER *HIS* TOMB!

THE AIR WILL BE CLEAR BY MORNING. PUT A GUARD ON TONIGHT.

SOMEONE YOU CAN *TRUST*.

I'LL GUARD THE TOMB MYSELF, SIR.

GOOD. BE SURE YOU'RE ARMED!

HOWOO - OOO - OOOOOOO

RASHID...! RASHID...!

PIERRE, HAVE YOU SEEN RASHID?

NO. WHY? —ISN'T HE HERE?

COME ON!

MON DIEU!

OH, WOW! THE MUMMY'S GONE!

HE CLIMBED OUT OF HIS COFFIN AND GOT RASHID!

YOU'LL MEET HIM AGAIN IN HEAVEN, NED.

THEN HE'S IN PARADISE?

IF KHA LET HIM GO. AFTER HE ROSE FROM HIS COFFIN AND KILLED RASHID!

RASHID WAS A MOSLEM, HENRY.

YES— MOST CERTAINLY.

HENRY— LISTEN— THOSE THINGS I TOLD YOU...

...ABOUT MUMMIES COMING TO LIFE— I'M AFRAID I...

TOLD LIES?

...EXAGGERATED. I OFTEN TELL STORIES. IT— IT'S SOMETHING I DO. TO MAKE LIFE SEEM MORE EXCITING—MORE WORTHWHILE.

BE CAREFUL NOT TO DISTURB ANYTHING.

LOOK, HENRY—A BUST OF KHA! THAT'S WHAT HE LOOKED LIKE.

"I WAS BELOVED OF THE PHARAOH. FOR MY SERVICE... HE GAVE ME...THE PRECIOUS STANDARD...BEARING THE SACRED JACKAL...WITH EYES OF FIRE..."

THERE'S NO JACKAL ON THIS STANDARD.

AHA! WAIT...

SOMETHING WAS HERE. IT'S BEEN BROKEN OFF...STOLEN!

AT LAST! A MOTIVE!

THIS IS PROBABLY WHAT IT LOOKED LIKE...

IT'S AN *IMPORTANT ARTIFACT* AND BELONGS IN A *MUSEUM*, HENRY!

SO RASHID'S MURDER WAS JUST A SMOKE-SCREEN—TO COVER THE ROBBERY?

YES. THE "EYES OF FIRE" ARE PROBABLY PRECIOUS STONES.

BUT WHO MOVED THE *MUMMY?* A NATIVE WOULDN'T. TOO SACRED!

ONE OF THE EUROPEAN ASSISTANTS?

—OR SOMEONE WITH A FOOT IN BOTH WORLDS.

WHO KNEW THE CURSE, BUT DIDN'T BELIEVE IT. WHO NEEDED MONEY—AND HATED RASHID!

MR. GHALY! NED—WILL YOU ARREST HIM?

NO PROOF, HENRY! EVIDENCE. LIKE THIS POWDER FROM RASHID'S BODY.

LOOKS LIKE MAGNESIUM.

PHOTOGRAPHER'S FLASH POWDER!

I WAS DREAMING ABOUT THAT MUMMY—SHUFFLING AROUND OUT THERE, WHEN...

MMMPF...

EASY...

NED!

SHHH! I NEED YOUR HELP, OLD LAD. I'M GOING TO SEARCH PIERRE'S TENT.

HE'LL *KILL* YOU!

NO—HE'S IN THE MESS TENT! I CAN SEE HIM.

I WANT *YOU* TO KEEP YOUR EYE SKINNED. IF HE MOVES—COME QUICK AND TELL ME!

EEE YEE-I-I-I-EEE-AGH!

THUD

OH, MY *GOD!* *PIERRE!*

HE'LL *KILL* ME!

HAA-ALP! HE'S GOING TO *KILL ME!*

HAA-HA! I CAN TELL YOU, KIDS. I'VE NEVER, *EVER* BEEN *THAT* SCARED —BEFORE OR SINCE!

JEEZ, OLD MAN— DON'T STOP *NOW!*

WHAT HAPPENED? *WHAT HAPPENED?*

NO - O - O! IT'S *PIERRE!* HE'S GOING TO *KILL* ME! JUST LIKE HE KILLED *RASHID!*

ARE YOU *CRAZY?*

WH...?! MR. LAWRENCE! TELL HIM—I DIDN'T KILL RASHID!

NO? THEN WHAT ARE YOU DOING HERE?

TAKING PHOTOGRAPHS —FOR THE NEWSPAPERS!

A MAN MUST LIVE! THEY PAY WELL FOR THIS SORT OF STORY!

THERE WAS MAGNESIUM POWDER ON RASHID'S BODY. YOUR *FLASH* POWDER, PIERRE...

I'M NOT THE ONLY ONE IN CAMP WHO USES...

NED! LOOK WHAT I FOUND. ISN'T IT A DYNAMITE PLUNGER?

DEMETRIOS!

THE HANDLE FITS HIS DETONATOR, ALL RIGHT.

MAGNESIUM POWDER!

HE'LL BE AT PORT SAID BY NOW, READY TO BOARD A SHIP.

NOT IF *I* CAN HELP IT!

WONDERFUL MEETING YOU, HENRY! YOU'RE A SPLENDID CHAP! I'LL WRITE! PROMISE — DON'T FORGET ME!

NED— DON'T GO! NED!

"DON'T FORGET ME," HE SAID. AS IF I EVER COULD!

HE WAS A HERO, EVEN THEN.

WELL, WHAT HAPPENED THEN...?

HUH... WHAT?

DID LAWRENCE CATCH THE KILLER?

WHEN HE GOT TO THE PIER, THE STEAMER WAS FIVE MINUTES GONE—AND DEMETRIOS WITH IT!

THE BAD GUY GOT AWAY?!

WHAT'D YOU DO?

ME? I WENT BACK TO CAIRO WITH MISS SEYMOUR, REJOINED MY PARENTS AND CONTINUED OUR TRIP!

WHAAT! IS THAT ALL THERE IS? WHAT ABOUT THE JACKAL?

C'MON, MISTER! TELL US THE REST —PLEASE!

ALL RIGHT—OKAY! BUT I HAVE TO GET HOME TO FEED HENRY. HE'S MY CAT. VERY FUSSY CAT—MAKES MY LIFE HELL SOMETIMES.

ANYWAY, EIGHT YEARS LATER, WHEN I WAS IN MEXICO...

WHAT HAS *MEXICO* GOT TO DO WITH IT?

Y-YOU, SIR.

LISTEN, KID. WHO'S TELLING THIS STORY— YOU OR ME?

DAMN RIGHT! SO SHUT UP AND LISTEN! NOW WHERE WAS I?

IN MEXICO.

MEXICO? WHAT WAS I DOING IN MEXICO? OH, YES. IT WAS SPRING BREAK.

I WAS VISITING COUSIN FRANK IN SANTA FE. I STILL HAD A WEEK TO GET BACK TO SCHOOL—SO WE HITCHED DOWN TO THE BORDER FOR SOME FUN—KNOW WHAT I MEAN?—WITH THE SEÑORITAS.

HOT SPOTS, YOU ASK?

LET'S SEE...*SPPUTT*...THAR'S CASA CALIENTE...'N' OLD CHILLIES. I DUNNO ...MAYBE *TOO* HOT FOR YOU BOYS.

GEE, THANKS, SOLDIER!

WATCH OUT FOR OL' CHILLIES. YOU'RE LIABLE TO...

KRAK

HUHN...?

HEE-I-I-AAA!

ENOUGH BLOODSHED! I'M *SICK* OF IT! WE ARE SOLDIERS, HEROES—NOT *ASSASSINS!*

PUT DOWN YOUR WEAPONS —OR SHOOT ME, TOO!

WHO'S THAT?

GENERAL FRANCISCO VILLA.

PANCHO VILLA?!

OUI!

TU AS DE LA CHANCE, MON VIEUX!

A FRENCHMAN— RIDING WITH VILLA?

HEY, MAN, HOW COME YOU CAN RAP IN ALL THOSE FOREIGN LANGUAGES? SPANISH, FRENCH 'N' ALL...

SOMETHING MR. LAWRENCE HAD TOLD ME, OUT THERE ON THE DESERT...

WHEREVER YOU GO, HENRY, LEARN THE LANGUAGE! IT'S THE KEY THAT UNLOCKS *EVERYTHING!*

HE WAS RIGHT. I'VE LEARNED QUITE A FEW. ANYHOW, THAT'S HOW I MET *REMY.* TURNED OUT HE WAS BELGIAN... MOST OF 'EM SPEAK FRENCH, YOU KNOW...

...WELL, NO SOONER DID THEY UNTIE ME THAN BAD NEWS ARRIVED!

MY GENERAL—THE YANKEE PERSHING IS CROSSING THE BORDER WITH AN *ARMY!*

VILLA WAS ON THE MOVE —AND I WAS TIED UP AGAIN.

MIRA! A YANQUI PLANE!

SCATTER! *GRENADES!*

DARN! I'M GOING TO MISS SCHOOL— FOR SURE!

GENERAL PERSHING, VILLA'S COLUMN IS ABOUT 40 MILES TO THE SOUTH.

HE'LL CIRCLE EAST, HEAD FOR THE MOUNTAINS. MOVE OUT, GENTLEMEN—

— I'M GOING TO TEACH VILLA WHAT IT MEANS TO INVADE THE UNITED STATES. I'M GOING TO *NAIL* THE SONOFA...!

CAREFUL WITH THAT! YOU WANT TO BLOW YOURSELVES UP, DO IT SOMEWHERE ELSE!

WHAT OTHER THINGS?

OUR CHILDREN STARVE. PRESIDENT CARRANZA... THE RICH ...THEY HAVE TAKEN EVERYTHING. SOLD HALF OUR COUNTRY TO YOU GRINGOS.

WE ARE SLAVES IN OUR OWN LAND. WHAT ELSE BUT TO FIGHT? FIGHT FOR *JUSTICE!*

WRONG!

THIS IS WHAT WE FIGHT FOR!

THE RIGHT TO OWN A PIECE OF IT, TO RAISE CROPS, FEED OUR CHILDREN! *THIS* IS OUR REVOLUTION—

A POOR HANDFUL OF DIRT,

NOW GO HOME, GRINGO—TO YOUR FAT, RICH LAND. GO HOME, BOY! I SET YOU FREE!

GENERAL! NO—

I WANT TO FIGHT FOR THE REVOLUTION!

GIVE THIS KID A JOB!

THAT'S THE LAST ONE.

CLAW! SOMETHING ABOUT THAT GUY WAS BOTHERING ME.

HMM—A PRE-COLOMBIAN COLLECTION? AND...HEY! WHAT WAS THIS?

AHA! I KNEW THAT PHOTO. I HAD WATCHED PIERRE TAKE IT— IN *EGYPT!*

WHEN CARDENAS LEFT...

ALL CLEAR, DEMETRIOS!

OKAY!

?!

I'VE FOUND HIM, LAWRENCE!

I'VE FOUND HIM —AT LAST!

HOW MUCH LONGER DO WE HAVE TO SIT HERE?

UNTIL ROBLES BRINGS NEWS OF THE TRAIN.

WHAT'S SO IMPORTANT ABOUT THIS TRAIN?

IT IS THE KEY TO CIUDAD GUERRERO.

ARE THEY CRAZY? THAT PLACE IS CRAWLING WITH FEDERALES! WE'LL GET OUR BUTTS SHOT OFF!

TEQUILA!

REMEMBER, BELGIAN—DON'T LIGHT THE FUSE UNTIL YOU'RE RIGHT *ON TOP OF* THE WALL!

BUT, GENERAL VILLA, THE TRACK DOES NOT GO NEAR ENOUGH...

I GREW UP HERE! THERE IS A *SPUR LINE* THAT RUNS RIGHT *INTO* THE WALL.

I WILL *SWITCH* THE TRACKS AND SEND THE TRAIN *CRASHING* INTO IT!

ONCE WE'RE THROUGH THAT WALL, THE CITY WILL BE OURS! HURRY!

WHEN I UNCOUPLE THIS FLATCAR, STAY CLEAR, INDIANA!

WHAT IF JOSE *CAN'T* SWITCH THE TRACKS?

THEN WE *ALL* DIE!

SOUND THE ALERT! *EXPLOSIVES!*

OMIGOD! THE TRAIN'S ALMOST HERE! I'M TOO LATE...THEY'VE UNCOUPLED THE FLATCAR...AND I'M TOO LATE!

THOOM

VIVA VILLA!

THE MONEY STOREHOUSE, MY GENERAL!

BLOW IT OPEN!

KA-VOOM

?

KA-VOOM

A TERRIBLE THOUGHT WAS DAWNING ON ME. I MIGHT HAVE TO *KILL* SOMEBODY. *COULD I?*

BLAM

I—I'M SORRY, SIR. I DIDN'T MEAN TO...

WAP

VILLA WAS AS GOOD AS HIS WORD.

HE TOOK BABICORA, HEARST'S FABULOUS HACIENDA.

AND LET HIS PISTOLEROS RUN WILD. IT WASN'T PRETTY.

WHAT IS IT, INDIANA? ARE YOU ILL?

NOT EXACTLY! I... JUST DON'T KNOW IF THIS IS *MY* REVOLUTION!

If I should fall in battle, my last thought shall be of you!

THE HACIENDA HAD EVERYTHING ...EVEN A PRIVATE MOVIE HOUSE...

AH ☆ SIGH ☆ POBRECITA... SO SAD!

COMPLETE WITH NEWSREELS.

Two years of mighty conflict. Europe still locked in deadly struggle.

I LEAVE AT FIRST LIGHT. BE READY TO RIDE.

ONE THING I MUST DO FIRST.

IF YOU'RE NOT HERE AT DAWN, I LEAVE WITHOUT YOU.

AS YOU CAN GUESS, THERE W... SOMETHING I HAD TO FIND.

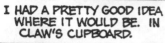

I HAD A PRETTY GOOD IDEA WHERE IT WOULD BE. IN CLAW'S CUPBOARD.

SURE ENOUGH! RIGHT BEHIND HIS MONEY BAGS!

WOW— EXACTLY AS NED DREW IT! ONLY THE RUBIES...THE *EYES* OF *FIRE* —ARE *GONE!*

CRUNCH

REMEMBER ME, DEMETRIOS?

I'M A FRIEND OF RASHID —THE MAN YOU *KILLED!*

I NEARLY MISSED MEETING UP WITH REMY.

BUT I MADE IT. WE WERE ON OUR WAY TO ENLIST IN THE GREAT WAR.

THAT'S IT. GOT TO GET BACK AND FEED HENRY!

MR. JONES—WH-WHAT HAPPENED TO THE... THE *JACKAL*?!

THE JACKAL? LOOK BEHIND YOU!

GIFT OF THE EGYPTIAN GOVERNMENT IN HONOR OF Professor Henry Jones, Jr.

WOW !!!

FINIS